ME & YOU

A Mother-Daughter Album

Lisa Thiesing

Hyperion Books for Children
New York

Printed in the United States of America.

3 5 7 9 10 8 6 4 2

This book is set in 24-point Hadriano Light.
The artwork for this book was prepared
using watercolor and pen and ink.

Thiesing, Lisa.
Me and you : a mother-daughter album / by Lisa Thiesing.—1st ed.
p.   cm.
Summary: A mother explains how much her daughter is like she was as a little girl.
ISBN 0-7868-0358-4 (trade).—ISBN 0-7868-2338-0 (library)
[1. Identity—Fiction. 2. Mothers and daughters—Fiction.]
I. Title.
PZ7.T3418Me   1997
[E]—dc21

97-27986
CIP
AC

To my family—
for memories lost and found
—L. T.

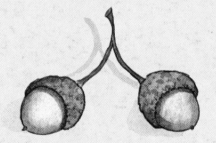

me   you

When I was a little baby,
I looked just like you.

I burped

and glurped

and pooped,

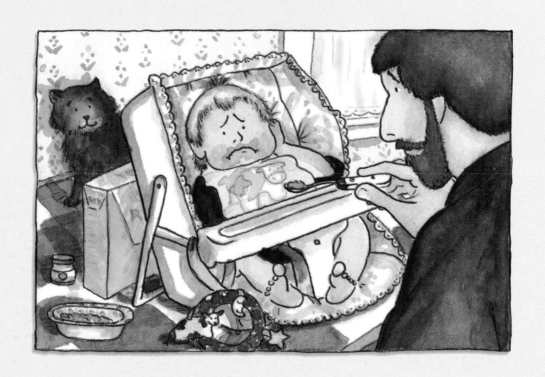

just like you.

I slept and played,
crawled and splashed,

just like you.

I had a mother and father
who loved me very much,

just like you.

I loved animals,

just like you.

And, just like you,
I hated the vacuum cleaner, having my hair
combed, and kisses (except on boo-boos).

I didn't like certain foods,

just like you.

Just like you, I liked being on top of things . . .

and getting to the bottom of things.

I loved
my friends, my baby-sitters,
and my relatives,

just like you.

I wanted to choose my own clothes,

just like you.

I loved to dance,

just like you.

I liked curtains,

just like you.

Just like you, I wasn't always good
and I wasn't always bad.

I was just learning to be me,
just like you are learning to be you.

And when I grew up,
I wanted to have a little girl . . .

just like you!